Stella AND THE Night Sprites
Knit-Knotters

By Sam Hay

Illustrated by Turine Tran

BRANCHES™

SCHOLASTIC INC.

Read all about
Stella AND THE Night Sprites!

Table of Contents

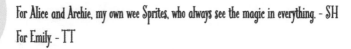

For Alice and Archie, my own wee Sprites, who always see the magic in everything. - SH
For Emily. - TT

Text copyright © 2016 by Sam Hay
Illustrations copyright © 2016 by Scholastic Inc.

All rights reserved. Published by Scholastic Inc., *Publishers since 1920.* SCHOLASTIC, BRANCHES, and associated
logos are trademarks and/or registered trademarks of Scholastic Inc.

The publisher does not have any control over and does not assume any responsibility for author or
third-party websites or their content.

No part of this publication may be reproduced, stored in a retrieval system, or transmitted in any form or
by any means, electronic, mechanical, photocopying, recording, or otherwise, without written permission
of the publisher. For information regarding permission, write to Scholastic Inc., Attention: Permissions
Department, 557 Broadway, New York, NY 10012.

This book is a work of fiction. Names, characters, places, and incidents are either the product of the
author's imagination or are used fictitiously, and any resemblance to actual persons, living or dead,
business establishments, events, or locales is entirely coincidental.

Library of Congress Cataloging-in-Publication Data
Hay, Sam, author.
Knit-knotters / by Sam Hay.
pages cm. — (Stella and the night sprites ; 1)
Summary: Stella discovers that her new glasses are magic, allowing her to see the knit-knotters
— night sprites that are flitting around town tying knots in children's hair so they need haircuts
— and when a conversation with one of them, Trixie, reveals the reason, Stella comes up with a
plan to deal with the mischievous fairies.
ISBN 0-545-81998-9 (pbk.) — ISBN 0-545-81999-7 (hardcover) — ISBN 0-545-82004-9
(ebook) — ISBN 0-545-82005-7 (eba ebook)
1.Fairies — Juvenile fiction. 2. Eyeglasses — Juvenile fiction. 3. Magic — Juvenile fiction. 4.
Hair — Juvenile fiction. [1. Fairies--Fiction. 2. Eyeglasses — Fiction. 3. Magic--Fiction. 4.
Hair — Fiction.] I. Title.
PZ7.1.H39Kn 2016
813.6 — dc23 [Fic]
2014041878

ISBN 978-0-545-81999-2 (hardcover)/ISBN 978-0-545-81998-5 (paperback)

10 9 8 7 6 5 4 3 2 1   16 17 18 19 20

Printed in China   38
First edition, January 2016
Illustrated by Turine Tran
Edited by Katie Carella
Book design by Liz Herzog

New Look

The bell above the door jangled as Stella and her mom steppcd inside.

Stella tried to feel brave. But her tummy was doing somersaults.

This was Stella's second trip to the eyeglass shop. A few days ago, Dr. Bruce had done Stella's eye exam. She had made it really fun.

First, she'd asked Stella to read letters on a chart. The letters started **BIG** then got really small.

Next, Dr. Bruce had given her a pair of red-and-green glasses to wear. They made a few of the letters go *blurry*.

Then Stella had tried on a thick pair of glasses with lots of different lenses.

Some lenses made everything wonky.

Others made everything clear. Really clear.

So it wasn't the eye doctor Stella was worried about. Secretly, it had felt good to see better. But Stella wasn't sure she wanted glasses. Not even the pretty purply-pink ones that she had picked out with her mom.

"Hi, Stella," said Dr. Bruce from the back of the shop. "I'm finishing up with another customer. Here are your glasses." She gave Stella a hard purple box. "Take a look. I'll be back soon to make sure they fit."

Stella held the box in her hands. She felt too nervous to open it.

Mom looked at the clock. "While you're waiting, I'll go next door to make you an appointment at the new hair salon." Mom ruffled Stella's hair. "Too long. And too full of tangles!"

"Tangles?" Stella ran her fingers through her hair. Or at least she tried to. *"Ow!"* She winced. Mom was right. It was super-knotty.

Stella frowned. "But, Mom—" she began, a bubble of worry growing in her tummy.

Her mom was already out the door.

Stella stared at the hard box in her hands. *If I get glasses,* she thought, *AND new hair, no one—not even my own family—will know it's me!*

A Touch of Magic

Stella sat down to wait. She looked around. There were glasses everywhere. All shapes. All styles. Round, rectangular, clear, colorful . . .

Some had pointy edges. Others had no frames at all.

Just then, the bell above the door rang. Another customer came in.

Stella couldn't help staring. The lady's outfit looked like it had been in a fight with a paint box. Her top had purple spots on it. Her skirt was orange zigzags. Her tights were candy canes: bright red and white stripes. And she smelled like strawberries.

"Hello." The lady smiled at Stella. "Are you getting glasses today?"
Stella nodded.

"Me, too." The lady sighed. "Can you believe it? I've had 78 years of good eyesight and all of a sudden my eyes are letting me down!" She blinked a few times, as if she were telling them off.

She had 78 years of good eyesight? Stella frowned. *I can't believe she's that old.* The lady looked just like Stella's Aunt Lulu. And Stella knew Aunt Lulu was only 25—she'd gone to her birthday party last Saturday.

The lady stretched and yawned. Then she spun around a few times on her tiptoes. "It's probably my own fault," she said, coming to a stop. "Too many late nights poring over spell books with tiny print!" She winked at Stella.

Spell books? Stella wondered if the lady was teasing her.

"Achoo!" The lady sneezed. "Fairy dust!" she said. "It always gets up my nose."

Stella's eyes widened. *Did she really just say fairy dust?*

The lady peered into her big purse. "Now where did I put my handkerchief? Oh!"

The purse tipped over, scattering its contents.

"I'll get it!" Stella sprang up to catch a pen rolling across the floor. *"Oooooh,"* Stella said, holding it up. "This isn't a pen." It looked more like a long, golden chopstick. "What is it?" she asked.

"A wand," the lady said, taking it from Stella. "Gold wands are always the best, don't you think?"

"*Um.*" Stella didn't know what to say.

The lady tapped the thing on her other hand and little sparkles popped out the end.

Stella gasped.

The lady smiled and pointed to Stella's box. "Are those your glasses? May I see?"

Stella handed her the box.

"Oh, lovely," the lady said, peeking inside. "Look!" She turned the open box around so Stella could see, too.

"Huh?" Stella thought Dr. Bruce must have given her the wrong box. The glasses didn't look anything like she remembered. They were WAY prettier. And glittery, too!

"Try them on," the lady said.

The glasses felt warm in Stella's hands—and as light as cobwebs. It was as though they'd been spun by sparkly spiders.

Stella put on the glasses. She looked around the room. "So bright!" she said.

Just then, Stella's mom walked back into the shop. And Dr. Bruce came out of the office. Stella expected them both to say how different her new glasses looked. But they didn't seem to notice.

"Stella, you look so pretty," Mom said.
"Your glasses fit well," Dr. Bruce added.
"You look beautiful!" the lady said.

Stella smiled up at the lady through her new glasses. She spotted something odd: The lady had a silvery glow around her!

Eye Spy!

Stella didn't want to take off her new glasses on the ride home.

The grass shone brighter.

The sky looked bluer.

And there was so much more to see.

"Baby squirrels!" She pressed her face against the window. "Look, Mom! They're playing hide-and-seek in the trees."

Stella saw other things, too.

A garden full of golden sunflowers. Their big heads bobbed in the breeze. A bright bird, with the glossiest wings ever. Even the old gray road sparkled in the sunshine.

"Wait until Josh and Dad and Pepper see you!" Stella's mom said.

"Oh . . . *um* . . . yeah." Stella stopped smiling.

Josh was her older brother. What if he laughed at her glasses?

What if Dad thought she looked silly?

What if Pepper, their dog, didn't want to play with her anymore?

Stella suddenly felt nervous again.

Mom pulled into their driveway. "We're home!" she said.

Maybe I can hide my glasses, Stella thought.

She was just about to take them off when she saw Dad and Josh waiting on the porch. They waved to her.

Too late, Stella thought, touching her new glasses. *They've seen me now.*

Stella took a deep breath. Then she climbed out of the car.

Night Light

Josh did *not* laugh at Stella's glasses. He actually said something sort of nice. "You look okay, I guess," he said.

And Dad *didn't* think Stella's glasses looked silly. "You're getting so grown-up," he said, hugging her tight.

Pepper didn't even notice. *"Whooaa!"* Stella giggled as Pepper jumped up to say hi. "No, Pepper! My glasses *don't* need a wash!"

The best thing about having glasses was reading time.

Before Stella got her glasses, her eyes used to get SO tired as soon as she tried to read in bed—she had to squint to see better. Not anymore.

"Lights-out time," Mom said, coming into Stella's room.

"Aw, Mom," Stella said. "I'm not sleepy."

"Good night, Stella." Mom took her book and her glasses, and put them by her bed. "Don't forget we're going to the hair salon in the morning."

Stella groaned. She'd forgotten about getting her hair cut. Stella waited until she heard Mom go downstairs, then . . .

"Got it!" she said, pulling her flashlight out from under her pillow. She grabbed her book and her glasses, too. *Mom won't see my light under here!* Stella thought, tugging the covers over her head.

She read six whole pages before her eyes began to droop. *I should take off my glasses,* Stella thought as her eyes started to shut. *But I'm just too sleepy.*

A moment later, her eyes snapped open! She'd heard a noise in her room.

Stella wriggled. Her book was squished under her arm. The flashlight batteries had run out. And she was still wearing her glasses.

The room smelled like strawberries. It reminded Stella of the lady in the shop.

Just then, she saw a tiny bright light dart through the air!

Stella blinked and tried to rub her eyes. But as she did, she knocked her glasses off. "Oh!" The light vanished.

She pushed her glasses back on. The light reappeared. *Weird,* she thought.

Stella stared at the tiny light. *What is that? A bug, maybe? A moth? A firefly?*

Stella had seen fireflies at summer camp. But never inside her house.

Then the light dived down and fluttered past her nose.

Whooaa! Stella breathed in.

It wasn't a bug. It was a tiny girl!

Stella gasped.

5

Seeing Is Believing

The tiny girl had curly blue hair, a shiny purple skirt, and silver butterfly wings on her back. Her wings were beating so fast they were blurry.

Stella froze. Her mouth felt dry. She didn't want to move, to breathe, to blink, in case the creature disappeared.

Is she the Tooth Fairy? Stella wondered. One of her teeth was a bit wobbly. But Stella didn't think it was ready to fall out yet.

The girl darted across the ceiling, scattering small sparks in the air. Stella looked around the room trying to keep track of her. Then Stella felt a tug on her head. *Hey!* Something was pulling her hair. HARD!

Keeping really still, Stella glanced up.

The tiny girl was hovering above her head, with a clump of Stella's hair in her hands. Wait. It looked like she was knitting. And she was using Stella's hair instead of yarn!

Then the girl tugged a strand of Stella's hair WAY too hard—worse even than when Mom combed it for school.

"Stop that!" Stella reached up and grabbed the girl. She cupped her inside her hands.

"Let me go! Let me go!" shouted a small, squeaky voice. The creature fluttered angrily. Something sharp pricked Stella's skin.

"Ow!" Stella opened her hand.

The girl poked her again with one of her knitting needles. "You squished me!" she squeaked. "Look!" She 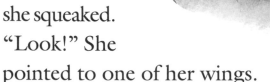 pointed to one of her wings.

It did look a bit bent.

"Well, you pulled my hair!" Stella said.

"That's my job!"

"Huh?"

"I'm a knit-knotter," the girl said, tossing her curly blue hair. "You're not supposed to be able to see me!"

Stella just stared at the tiny girl.

"No one's ever seen me before," the girl said. "So how come you can?"

Stella felt her glasses grow warmer. They made her face tingle. She looked at the girl. She was glowing. She looked sort of silvery—like the lady in the shop. Stella gulped. Her tummy felt tight. Her heart thumped against her chest.

Could this amazing tiny creature be real?

A thought was forming in her mind . . .

"Wait a minute," Stella said. She slipped her glasses off. The tiny girl vanished. Stella put them back on. The girl reappeared. "*Whoa.* These must be *magic* glasses!"

6
Knit Wit

The girl stamped her foot and shook her hair. Warm glittery sparkles fell on Stella's hand. "Well, this is not going to work!" the girl said. "How can I tie knots in your hair if you can see me?"

Stella frowned. "Why do you want to tie knots in my hair?"

"I told you. I'm a knit-knotter," the girl said. "That's what knit-knotters do. We tie knots in children's hair!"

"That's mean!" Stella said. "Knots hurt!"
The girl looked puzzled. "They do?"

"Yeah. Knots make my hair all tuggy," Stella explained. "When Mom combs the knots out of my hair, it hurts."

"Oh." The girl's silvery face turned red. She looked at her feet. "*Um* . . . well, I'm sorry," she said.

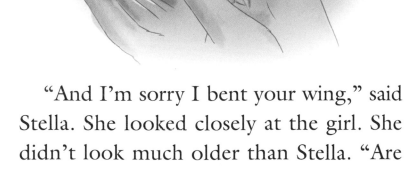

"And I'm sorry I bent your wing," said Stella. She looked closely at the girl. She didn't look much older than Stella. "Are you a fairy?"

"No!" The girl puffed out her chest. "I am a night sprite. We are much more fun!"

"What's a *night sprite?*" Stella asked.

"We're like fairies—only better." The sprite shook her wings, and the dent popped out of the bent one. "We come out when it gets dark. And we do all the fun stuff that fairies don't. We put sticky yellow **wax-packs** in your ears. And we stuff **pong-papers** inside your big brother's

sneakers, so they stink real bad! *Pee-yew!*" The sprite held her nose and giggled.

Stella's eyes widened.

"We hide marker caps, too," the sprite said, "so the colors dry out."

Stella gasped. She had lots of markers without lids. It was SO annoying when they dried out.

"Sometimes we hide your socks," the sprite went on, "so you can never find a pair. And we paint dust-must on your treasures."

Stella looked at her shelves. The little china dogs she collected did look dusty.

"Then there are the *finger-dippers*," the girl said.

"The what?"

"The finger-dippers. They're night sprites who paint mud on your nails, so it looks like you never wash your hands. *Hee-hee!*"

Stella folded her arms. "Night sprites are mean."

"Huh?" The sprite stopped smiling. "B-b-b-but these things are just jokes." Her bottom lip wobbled. "We're only having fun. We do other stuff, too! Watch!"

A bright rainbow
shot up and over
Stella's head. The
bright colors
made her blink.

"Wow!" Stella
breathed.

"And watch this!"
the sprite said.

Pink flowers burst out of the carpet. Their
silky flower petals unfolded, one by one.

"Cool!" Stella whispered.

"And this!" The sprite giggled again.

Large cotton candy clouds floated down from the ceiling. Stella caught one.

"*Mmm,*" she said, taking a bite. "This cloud tastes yummy."

Stella stopped chewing and sighed. "But tying knots in people's hair is not fun."

POP! The rainbow vanished.

POP! The flowers disappeared.

POP! The clouds melted away to nothing.

"It's not?" the sprite asked.

"No!" Stella said. "Because of you, I have to get my hair cut tomorrow. Mom says it's *so* full of tangles that it needs a chop."

"Oops." The sprite gulped.

"I like my hair just the way it is," Stella said. "I don't want to get it cut."

"I guess that *is* my fault," said the sprite. She sniffed sadly. "But if I don't tie knots in your hair, then I won't get the big prize!"

Stella frowned. "There's a prize for tying knots in my hair?" she asked.

The sprite nodded.

"Really?" Stella scratched her ear. *What sort of person gives prizes for tying knots in hair?*

A Knotty Problem

The sprite shuffled around on Stella's hand. She seemed nervous. "*Um* . . . Well, you see," she began, "there's this **hairy-fairy** named Mary who owns that new hair salon in town—"

"What's a hairy-fairy?" Stella interrupted. "Is she a very hairy fairy? Like a Bigfoot fairy?"

The sprite giggled. "Nope. Hairy-fairies look a lot like humans," explained the sprite. "They don't have wings, and they are really big. They also like to style hair."

"Okay," Stella said.

"But Mary the hairy-fairy has a problem. She hasn't had enough customers in her hair salon lately. So she made a deal with the knit-knotters."

"What sort of deal?" Stella asked.

"A really good deal," the sprite said. Her eyes sparkled emerald green. "Every knit-knotter in town must tie a thousand knots by tomorrow. Then Mary will give each of us a big prize—a fairy bracelet!"

"A thousand knots?" Stella said. "So tomorrow morning, lots of kids will wake up with knotty hair just like mine?"

"Yes," said the sprite proudly. "They'll all need a trip to the hair salon for a chop! And Mary will make lots of money."

"That's awful!" Stella said.

"It is?" The sprite seemed confused. "Well, I'm exhausted. I still have ten heads to do before dawn." She picked up her knitting needles. "Can I get on with your knots now?"

"No!" Stella clamped her hands over her head.

"But I *have* to," the sprite moaned. "I won't get my bracelet if I don't."

Stella thought really hard. She scratched her ear the way she always did when she was thinking. "How will this hairy-fairy *know* if you've knotted a thousand knots?"

"Because every time I tie a knot, a sparkly bow appears on my wings!" The sprite turned around and fluttered her silvery wings.

There were so many sparkly bows Stella couldn't count them.

"I have 945 bows," the sprite said. "Only 55 to go! I've been collecting them all week. I did half your head last night. And I came back tonight to finish the job. You have such lovely hair." She picked up a strand of Stella's hair and wrapped it around her needles. "But you move too much while you sleep. Silly human!" She giggled.

"Stop that!" Stella pulled her hair free. "No more knotting my hair!" She glanced around the room. *There had to be another way the sprite could earn her bows.* Stella looked at her toy box. "Oh!" she said. "I think I might have an idea."

Winging It

Stella slipped out of bed. She wasn't sure her idea would work, but it was worth a try.

"Over here!" Stella called. "By the way, I'm Stella. What's your name? We've been so busy chatting, I forgot to ask."

"Trixie!" the sprite said, fluttering across the room. "Because I love tricks!" She did three forward rolls, then *POP!* She was gone. She reappeared suddenly on Stella's shoulder. "Boo!"

Stella smiled. "Now, about my idea," she said, lifting the lid of her toy box. "Take a look in here."

Trixie peered over her shoulder. "*Oooh,* you have so many dolls!"

"I love dolls," Stella said.

Stella had lots of dolls. Small ones. Tall ones. A doll with long, pink, wavy hair. Another with braids. There was a doctor doll. And one in a Santa suit. Some could even cry and crawl by themselves.

Stella picked up a doll with long blonde hair. "What if you were to tie knots in my doll's hair instead of in mine?"

"Huh?" Trixie looked confused.

"Well, it would be much easier to do since dolls don't move," Stella said. "I just wonder if doll knots would make bows on your wings?"

Trixie shrugged. "I don't know. Let me try." Trixie picked up her needles, and worked a small stitch in the doll's hair.

Stella stared at Trixie's wings, her fingers crossed. *Come on, come on . . .*

"It worked!" Stella cried.
Trixie knitted another knot.
"There's another bow!" Stella called.

"More!" Trixie shouted, her wings shaking with excitement.

"Wait," Stella said. "First, go get your friends so we can show them the dolls. Then they can *all* tie knots on dolls' hair tonight."

Trixie frowned. "But what about the fairy bracelets?"

"You'll still get them," Stella said. "Mary the hairy-fairy told you to tie a thousand knots. But she didn't say *what* you had to tie them on!"

Trixie nodded. "*Um . . . yeaahh,*" she said, "but doll hair isn't as much fun as human hair. The other knit-knotters might not *want* to do this."

"Tell your friends that if they stick to dolls' hair tonight," Stella said, "then I'll make them each a necklace!"

"A necklace?" Trixie asked. "For every knit-knotter?"

"Yup." Stella picked up her bead box off her desk and opened it. "Look!"

Trixie's eyes widened. "You have the sparkliest beads I've ever seen."

Stella ran her hand through thousands of tiny speckles: gold, silver, bright pink, purple, green. "I love beads," she said.

"*Ooooh,*" Trixie said. "Night sprites love sparkles, too. Will you really share yours?"

Stella nodded. "I always share my sparkles with my friends."

Trixie hugged Stella's little finger. "I'll be back," she said.

There was a heart-shaped glitter burst just above Stella's hand. Trixie was gone.

Sprite Fright!

Stella climbed into bed with her bead box on her lap.

I wonder how many sprites will come, she thought.

She didn't have to wait long to find out.

There was a sudden blast of cool air. The smell of strawberries filled the room. Heart-shaped glitter bursts flashed all around.

A big group of sprites arrived at the same time. Some were talking. Others were singing. "Night sprites!" Stella whispered.

The sprites darted left and right. Racing and chasing. Stella tried to count them. But they moved too fast. *25, 26, 27 . . . oops!* Stella lost count again. There were so many sprites that the room was lit up by all their tiny lights. A purple-haired sprite buzzed past Stella's nose.

"Hello," Stella said.

The sprite giggled shyly.

"Hi!" Stella said in a louder voice. "My name is Stella."

There were more giggles. A few sprites came closer.

Stella couldn't stop staring. The sprites all looked different from one another. Some had long hair—right down to their tiny toes. Others had short hairdos with silver bells on the end. A few had their knitting needles tucked behind their ears. Others wore the needles in their hair like large bobby pins.

Their outfits were different, too. Shiny gold skirts. Silver spotty shirts. Shorts, jumpsuits, and big, floaty pants. Stella saw every color of the rainbow—and more!

"Ouch!" Stella gasped. A tiny sprite in a gold dress had tied a knot in Stella's hair.

"Hey!" Stella said as a pink-haired sprite tied a knot on the other side of her head.

"Stop that!" Stella cried. She shook her head and two green sprites fell out of her hair. *Where's Trixie?* Stella thought. *I can't hold these night sprites off much longer!*

A big blue bubble burst above Stella's head. All the sprites turned to look.

10

A Crafty Plan

"Trixie!" Stella yelled.

Trixie did three forward rolls in the air and landed on Stella's shoulder.

"I wanted to get the sprites' attention!" Trixie whispered. "Magic bubbles always make a really loud *POP!*"

"I'm so glad you came back," Stella said.

Trixie flew up closer to the sprites. "Stella is my friend," she told them. "So don't tie knots in her hair!"

"*Aww.*" A small sprite groaned.

"But that's our job!" a curly-haired sprite grumbled.

"Why did you bring us here then?" a green sprite asked.

"Yeah! How will we get our bracelets if we don't knit knots?" said the sprite in the gold dress.

"We *are* going to knit knots—but we're going to knit them in Stella's dolls' hair," Trixie said. "Dolls don't move around at all. And we still get our bows, so Mary will still give us our bracelets. I'll show you."

Trixie flew over to the toy box. She picked up a doll and did a quick knot in its hair.

PING!
A new bow appeared on her wings.
"*Ooooh,*" the sprites said.

"If you all knit knots only on dolls' hair tonight," Stella said, "then I will make each of you a beautiful necklace." She opened her bead box to show them.

The sprites crowded around.

"Lovely sparkles," a tiny sprite said.

"So shiny!" a pink-haired sprite said.

"Let's start knitting!" the sprite in the gold dress shouted.

The knit-knotters swarmed around the toy box. Their bright lights lit up the room.

Trixie fluttered back to Stella's shoulder. "They like your plan!"

"I'm so glad!" cried Stella. "Now," she said, settling back into bed, "I need to figure out how many necklaces to make."

She counted the sprites again. It was easier now that they had stopped flying around. She did the math in her head: *48, 49, 50.*

"Wow! I'll have to make 50 necklaces!" said Stella.

Trixie looked worried. "Can you do that?"

"I think so. These necklaces will be itty-bitty sprite-sized. So they won't take long to make."

"Yay!" Trixie called.

Stella smiled. Then an idea popped into her head. "Trixie, can I ask you something?"

"Sure."

"Could you untie the knots in my hair?" Stella asked. "I really don't want to have to get my hair cut tomorrow."

Trixie's cheeks turned pink. Her smile vanished. "No. *Um* . . . A knit-knotter can't undo knots."

"Really?"

Trixie shook her head. "We can only *tie* knots. I'm sorry, Stella."

"Oh, well. I guess I'll try brushing them out myself, then," Stella said.

A little pink bubble rose up out of Trixie's head.

The bubble popped. Her face lit up. "I just had an idea! I'll go get my friend Lucy."

"Lucy?" Stella said. "Is she a sprite, too?"

Trixie nodded. "She's a lace-puller!"

"A what?"

"She unties shoelaces," Trixie said. "You know, on sneakers."

Stella laughed. *Josh's laces are always coming undone,* she thought. *Is it because of Lucy?*

Trixie fluttered around Stella's hair. "Lucy could undo these knots in a jiffy."

"Really?"

"Sure!" Trixie wiggled her fingers. "She has teeny little hands—perfect for pulling out knots."

"Awesome!" Stella exclaimed.

"First, I'll tie some more knots on your dolls," Trixie said. "Then I'll go find Lucy."

"Thank you, Trixie," Stella said. "You're the best!"

Trixie blew Stella a kiss.

When the kiss landed on Stella's cheek, it tickled.

Trixie fluttered off to join all the other sprites at the toy box.

Stella picked up her bead thread. "I just hope I don't fall asleep," she said, yawning.

Chop Swap

$\mathcal{S}$tella? Stella! Wake up!"

Stella blinked. Mom was sitting on her bed with the bead box on her lap. The room was full of light. Daylight.

"Were you up late doing crafts?" Mom smiled. "You fell asleep with your glasses on." Mom picked up the flashlight. She clicked it on and off. "And this is out of power."

"Mom!" Stella said as she looked around the room. "The necklaces! Where are they?"

Mom checked the box. "Your bead box is empty, Stella. You must have shared your beads at Emily's sleepover last week."

"Oh, I forgot about Emily's sleepover." Stella's shoulders drooped. *So all those night sprites were just a dream?*

Mom smiled. "Don't worry. We can stop by the bead store after your haircut today."

Stella groaned. "My haircut!" She'd forgotten about getting her hair cut. "But, Mom—" Stella began.

"Now, Stella," Mom interrupted, "you know how knotty your hair has been lately. You need a trim!" Mom smoothed Stella's bangs off her face. "Oh," she said, looking puzzled. "Your hair doesn't feel so knotty today."

Stella ran her own fingers through her hair. Mom was right. Her hair felt silky soft. Stella gasped. *Maybe Lucy the lace-puller had untied the knots in my hair!*

"Mom, *um,* " Stella said. "I was thinking. Maybe I could get a haircut another day— now that my hair's not so tangly."

"Well," Mom said, "I guess I could do with a cut myself. Perhaps I could have your appointment. We could still go to the bead store after."

"YES! That's a great idea, Mom!"

"Okay, okay!" Mom laughed. "Don't squeeze me too tight!" Mom stood up. "Dad is making pancakes for breakfast. So you'd better hurry up or Josh will eat them all."

Stella jumped out of bed! She LOVED pancakes.

"Please clean up your room first. It's a mess!" Mom said, walking out.

Stella looked over at the toy box.

"Whooaa!"

The dolls were scattered across the floor. They looked like they'd been having a wild and crazy party.

Stella bent down to put the dolls back in the box.

"Oh!" she said, picking up a Rapunzel doll. It had the knottiest hair Stella had ever seen. *Thank goodness these knots aren't in* my *hair,* she thought. *Or I would for sure be going to the salon for a chop!*

Hairy-Fairy

Stella stared out the window on the ride into town. Everything still looked sharp and shiny and bright, thanks to her new glasses. But were they really magic? Stella touched them. *They don't feel magic,* she thought.

"Here we are," Mom said, pulling into the parking lot outside the hair salon.

Stella read the sign.

It said MARY'S CUTZ AND CURLZ in bright-pink letters.

Stella frowned. *Mary's Cutz and Curlz? Didn't Trixie say Mary was the name of the hairy-fairy?*

"Look," Mom said, stepping out of the car. "Something is happening over at the bead store."

Stella looked at the store next to the salon. Her eyes twinkled. "So many balloons!"

"They must be having a party," Mom said. "The sign says GRAND RE-OPENING! Someone new must have bought the store."

"Can we go in?" Stella asked.

"Soon," Mom said, entering the salon.

Mary's Cutz and Curlz had three chairs, three sinks, and a drier at the back. It smelled like lemon-shampoo bubbles. Stella and her mom were the only customers.

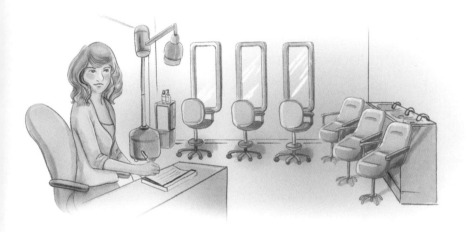

"Welcome, Mrs. Summers." A woman with bangs and a cranky face was sitting at the desk. "Is Stella ready for her haircut?"

"Hi," Mom said. "We've had a change of plan. I'm actually going to get *my* hair cut today."

Stella stared at the woman behind the desk. *Could she really be a hairy-fairy?*

Mary smiled. "I'd be happy to fit you *both* in!"

Mom shook her head. "No, I'll just be taking Stella's appointment. Her hair isn't as knotty as I'd thought."

"Really?" Mary glared at Stella. "Are you sure about that?"

Stella nodded. She blinked a few times. Mary had a strange, red, fuzzy glow around her. It made her look angry.

"You know, I expected to be very busy today. I thought *lots* of children would be coming. It's annoying when things don't turn out the way you planned!" Mary said.

Stella gasped. She looked around the empty salon. *Mary really was the hairy-fairy!* That meant Trixie and the night sprites were real, too. And the night sprites had tied knots on dolls' hair. Her plan HAD worked. None of it was a dream after all.

"This way," Mary said to Mom, leading her over to the sink.

"Stella," Mom called. "Why don't you go next door? I won't be long."

"Okay, Mom." Stella headed for the door. *I'll find the best beads ever,* she thought. She ran all the way.

"Wow!" Stella stopped just inside the bead store. She couldn't believe her eyes.

13

A Surprise in Store

Stella looked around the shop. There were beads everywhere! Rows and rows of the most amazing sparkles Stella had ever seen. Stars. Hearts. Pretty pink cat-shaped beads. Beads shaped like bubbles. And cakes. And candy. Tiny diamonds. Little pearls. The brightest rainbow beads ever.

Stella ran her hand through a big bin of gold stars. The beads glistened. *The sprites will love these,* she thought.

The smell of strawberries filled the air.

"Would you like a box to put your beads in?" said a voice behind her.

Stella turned. "Oh!" she cried. "It's you!"

The colorful lady from the eyeglass shop smiled at her. "Hello again."

Stella felt her glasses get warmer. Her face tingled.

"Welcome to my bead store," the lady said.

"*Your* bead store?" Stella asked.

"Yes," the lady said. "I just opened it this morning. How are your new glasses?"

"Awesome," Stella said. "How are *your* new glasses?"

"Wonderful!" The lady tapped the frame of her glasses. "I can see much better now."

"Me, too," Stella said. "You won't believe what I saw last night! There was this girl—a fairy girl. Well, a night sprite, actually. Her name is Trixie "

"Excuse me," said another customer. "I'm looking for wooden beads."

The lady turned to the customer. "The wooden beads are this way. Let me show you." She smiled at Stella. "I'll be back in a moment, honey."

"But I have to tell you—" Stella began.

Just then, Mom arrived. "So? What do you think? Do you like my new haircut?" Mom twirled around so Stella could see. "I think it's a bit spiky."

"*Um,* you look great, Mom," Stella said.

Mom's hair did look sort of spiky. But Stella did not want to hurt her feelings. "Look at all these amazing beads," Stella said, changing the subject.

The store began to fill up with customers. Stella didn't talk to the colorful lady again until she went to pay for the beads.

"You've picked out some beautiful beads," the lady said. She poured them into a glittery bag. "I'm sure your new little friends will love your sparkles, too!" She winked at Stella.

Sparkles? New little friends? Stella's glasses tingled. *The lady must have heard me telling her about Trixie, after all.*

"Here, take a balloon," the lady said. "Be sure to come back soon. Then you can tell me all about your adventures."

"I will!" Stella said. "Thank you."

And thank you for making my glasses magic, she thought.

As they left the store, Stella yawned. "Can I take a nap on the way home?"

"A nap?" Mom looked surprised.

"I'm a little tired," Stella explained.

"It must have been all that nighttime crafting," Mom said.

Stella nodded. *I need to get some sleep now in case Trixie comes back tonight!*

Sparkle Friends Forever

Much later, after Stella got ready for bed, she put all her new beads away. As she was putting the bead box back on her desk, she spotted something: a small purple envelope. It had a beautiful blue sparkle on the front. The sparkle shimmered when she picked it up. *Who is this from? How did it get here?* Stella wondered. She opened the envelope and a little blue bubble floated out.

"Huh?" Stella peered inside the bubble. She could see all of the knit-knotters. They were wearing the bead necklaces she had made for them!

POP! The bubble burst and a purple card fluttered out.

Dear Stella,

Thank you for the pretty necklaces. The knit-knotters love your sparkles!

See you again really soon!

Your friend,
Trixie xx

"Wow!" said Stella. She climbed into bed, her heart racing. She put Trixie's card under her pillow and made sure her glasses were on extra tight. "I'm ready, Trixie—ready for another peek into the magical world of the night sprites."

She turned off the light.

Must stay awake. Must not fall asleep, she told herself. But Stella's eyes were already starting to close . . .

Sam Hay didn't have to wear eyeglasses when she was a kid, but she always wanted a pair. Now she's got two—a blue pair and a purple sparkly pair, just like Stella's! Sam is sure there are night sprites living in her house because it's always such a mess! Maybe with her new eyeglasses, she'll spot a sprite soon ... Sam is the author of around 30 books for children, including the Undead Pets series. She lives in Wales.

Turine Tran illustrated more than fifteen fairy-tale books for children. At age nine, Turine thought that glasses would make her look smarter. But she never *needed* them. Today, Turine wears glasses similar to Stella's! But she doesn't need her glasses to see magic. Turine often sees sprites and she puts them into her drawings! When she is not busy drawing, she loves to travel! Turine lives in Singapore with four dogs.

Stella AND THE Night Sprites

~Knit-Knotters~

Questions and Activities

Why does Stella feel nervous at the eyeglass shop?

Glasses are awesome! Why are Stella's eyeglasses so special?

Ouch! Why does Trixie want to tie knots in Stella's hair?

Explain Stella's plan. What does she want Trixie and the other knit-knotters to do? Does the plan work?

There are many different types of night sprites. If you were a night sprite, which type of night sprite would you be? Write and draw your answer.